Mr. Reginald
and the Bunnies

Written and painted by Paula Wallace

To: Graham
From: Mimi & GranDad
Christmas 2019

Pomegranate Kids

PORTLAND, OREGON

Published by PomegranateKids®, an imprint of
Pomegranate Communications, Inc.
19018 NE Portal Way, Portland OR 97230
800 227 1428   www.pomegranate.com

Pomegranate Europe
Number 3 Siskin Drive
Middlemarch Business Park
Coventry CV3 4FJ, UK
+44 (0)24 7621 4461   sales@pomegranate.com

Pomegranate's mission is to invigorate, illuminate, and inspire through art.

To learn about new releases and special offers from Pomegranate, please visit www.pomegranate.com and sign up for our email newsletter. For all other queries, see "Contact Us" on our home page.

This product is in compliance with the Consumer Product Safety Improvement Act of 2008 (CPSIA) and any subsequent amendments thereto. A General Conformity Certificate concerning Pomegranate's compliance with the CPSIA is available on our website at www.pomegranate.com, or by request at 800 227 1428. For additional CPSIA-required tracking details, contact Pomegranate at 800 227 1428.

Library of Congress Control Number: 2017961167
ISBN 9780764981913

Pomegranate Item No. A273
Designed by Sophie Aschwanden
Printed in China

27 26 25 24 23 22 21 20 19 18   10 9 8 7 6 5 4 3 2 1

Mr. Reginald is a rabbit who lives under Mrs. Paddock's porch in a quiet neighborhood full of old houses. He has lived in his cozy home for a long time and is a perfect neighbor. Mr. Reginald is very tidy. He likes everything placed *just so*.

And, he's not at all noisy.

As headmaster, Mr. Reginald takes great pride in the Hutch School for Bunnies, but he was glad to be home for a spring holiday without students. No bunnies underfoot, no teachers complaining about all the work they had to do. It would be quiet, and everything would be *just so*.

When Mr. Reginald went to his mailbox on the last day of school, he found a letter from his sister. Imagine his surprise when he read her request.

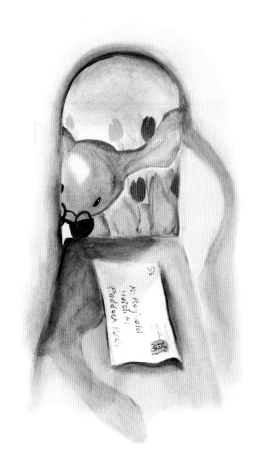

Dear Reginald,

   Would you mind having
Oliver, Mali, and P.D. come
for a visit during their
spring holiday?
   You'll find them quite helpful
and brave. They are not fussy
about food. In fact, they'll
eat just about everything.
                    Love,
                    Sis

Oh, great. Visitors,
he thought.

But when Mr. Reginald said "great," he did not mean *great*. He meant, *Oh no!*

As Mr. Reginald folded the letter, he imagined his sister's children—Oliver, Mali, and P.D.—bumbling and tumbling like wild animals in his tidy house. *They may be helpful and brave, but they will bounce on the furniture*, he thought. *They will always be hungry. They will never sleep.*

"Sweet Mother of Peter Rabbit," he said out loud. "What will I do about their noise?!"

He put the letter in his pocket and sighed. *I might as well get ready for the little dears.*

He set about bringing in extra food and pillows and towels.

Mrs. Paddock is Mr. Reginald's upstairs neighbor and a teacher at the Cottage School for Children. She has been looking forward to the spring holiday, when she could be in her garden. She loves her garden and every tool and bucket in her garden shed. She loves to arrange her plants and flowers and gardening tools *just so.* Spring holiday would mean no piles of homework to correct, no children bumbling and tumbling, no extra work from the principal—and it would be quiet!

It was the first day of holiday, and Mrs. Paddock was already busy in her garden. She was so busy, in fact, she did not notice three small, hungry rabbits arriving at Mr. Reginald's door.

When Mr. Reginald opened his door, the bunnies tumbled into his tidy hutch. They were so hungry after their bicycle ride that they ate EVERYTHING he had put on the table. They banged, bounced, and bumped into all the things that had been arranged *just so*. Poor Mr. Reginald was frazzled only minutes after the bunnies arrived!

"Why don't you go outside to play?" Mr. Reginald suggested when the bunnies offered to help with the washing up. "You will discover all sorts of things in Mrs. Paddock's garden."

Mr. Reginald took a deep breath as he filled the sink with every plate and cup he owned. All the towels were crumpled on the floor, too, and no one had even taken a bath.

Oliver, Mali, and P.D. bumbled out and bounced away. Oliver soon found Mrs. Paddock's laundry drying outdoors. Her apron waved in the breeze, and her red boots shone in the sun.

The three bunnies discovered they liked washday very much indeed! But Mrs. Paddock did not like finding her boots knocked over and her laundry rumpled about.

"How on earth did that happen?" Mrs. Paddock mumbled.

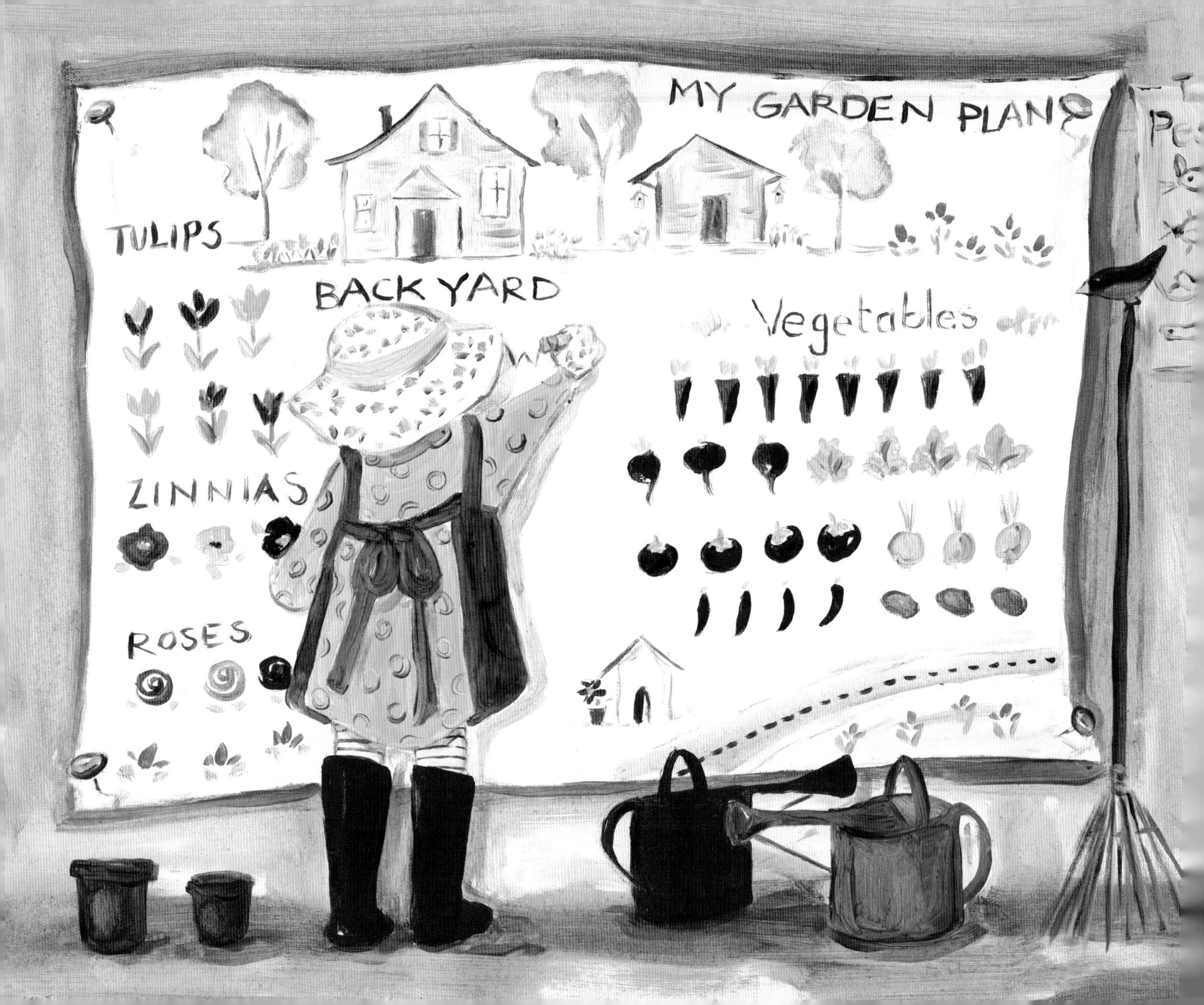
MY GARDEN PLANS
TULIPS
BACK YARD
Vegetables
ZINNIAS
ROSES

Mali wiggled her fluffy tail with delight when she discovered Mrs. Paddock's detailed garden maps drawn with rows and rows of flowers and vegetables. The bunnies liked maps, too, and they liked vegetables even more! But Mrs. Paddock did not like finding big bites taken out of all her lettuce and carrots.

"Who on earth could be eating my vegetables?!" she grumbled as she surveyed the mess in her garden.

P.D. munched on a lettuce sandwich while he watched Mrs. Paddock tend her garden until it was time to put things away. Mrs. Paddock kept all her tools and seeds and flowers to plant neatly stored *just so*. She knew exactly where everything was.

P.D. liked knowing exactly where everything was, too.

But when Mrs. Paddock stepped inside
the shed to return the watering can,

she stumbled on a carrot
the bunnies had dropped.

Aaaaaaaaah! she cried out
as she banged and bumbled
against the door . . .

and locked herself inside!

Oliver, Mali, and P.D. bounded to the shed door. They heard scary groans from within, and then Mrs. Paddock mumbled and grumbled, "How on earth did that carrot get there?! And wherever are my glasses? Oh dear me, I can't see!"

The bunnies took turns hopping as high as they could to reach the door handle, but it was too high.

They needed help!

I ♥ TULIPS

Mali could always run the fastest, so she raced to get Mr. Reginald.

"Oh no! Not one more thing!" Mr. Reginald exclaimed as he grabbed his jacket and hurried with his niece back to the garden shed.

The door handle was too high even for Mr. Reginald to reach, but if they worked together they might be able to rescue Mrs. Paddock. Mr. Reginald braced himself against the door *just so*. One by one the bunnies climbed onto one another's shoulders—higher than they had ever climbed before. They wobbled and bobbled until Mali could just reach the door handle. Together they pushed until the door started to budge, and . . .

everyone tumbled into the dark shed.

Mr. Reginald rushed to turn on the light while the three little bunnies hopped into action.

Oliver found Mrs. Paddock's glasses.

Mali peered into the fallen gardener's face and said, "Oh, that was scary! Did you hurt your head?"

P.D. added, "Would you like a carrot?"

The bunnies, you see, were quite helpful and brave, just as their mother had written—even if they were a bit bumbling and tumbling.

Later that evening, as Mrs. Paddock turned off the light to her garden shed and pulled the door closed, she saw that the bunnies had returned.

"Uncle Reginald said we could come out and check on you, 'cause we're not tired yet," P.D. said.

"Oh my," she said, and sighed as she rubbed the bump on her head.

I ♥ TULIP

Mrs. Paddock took the bunnies to her house and read to them from her favorite book. When she said good night, she let them take the storybook home to Mr. Reginald's hutch. *Now,* she thought, *all will be quiet.*

After Oliver, Mali, and P.D. had settled down, Mr. Reginald tucked them into bed. He was exhausted but proud of them. And once they were asleep, he could relax with his own book and everything would finally be *just so*.

About the Author

Artist and author Paula Wallace has been making art since her childhood days of Crayola crayons, Play-Doh, and Etch A Sketch. She studied art formally at the University of Iowa and pursued further training in Chicago and Ireland. In addition to fine art, Wallace has worked as an illustrator and muralist, set painter, art instructor, arts facilitator, and curator. Her art and stories are informed by her work with children and underserved communities, as well as by the urban and rural landscapes in which we dwell. Wallace has written and illustrated books for children and adults, and her fine art is in public and private collections around the world.